MARVEL
ANT-MAN

THE AMAZING ADVENTURES OF ANT-MAN

By Charles Cho

Inspired by Marvel's *Ant-Man*

Based on the Screenplay by Adam McKay & Paul Rudd

Story by Edgar Wright & Joe Cornish

Produced by Kevin Feige

Directed by Peyton Reed

LITTLE, BROWN AND COMPANY
New York Boston

marvelkids.com

Little, Brown and Company

Hachette Book Group
1290 Avenue of the Americas, New York, NY 10104
Visit us at lb-kids.com

Little, Brown and Company is a division of Hachette Book Group, Inc.
The Little, Brown name and logo are trademarks of Hachette Book Group, Inc.

The publisher is not responsible for websites (or their content) that are not owned by the publisher.

First Edition: June 2015

Library of Congress Control Number: 2015937500

ISBN 978-0-316-25669-8

10 9 8 7 6 5 4 3 2 1

CW

PRINTED IN THE UNITED STATES OF AMERICA

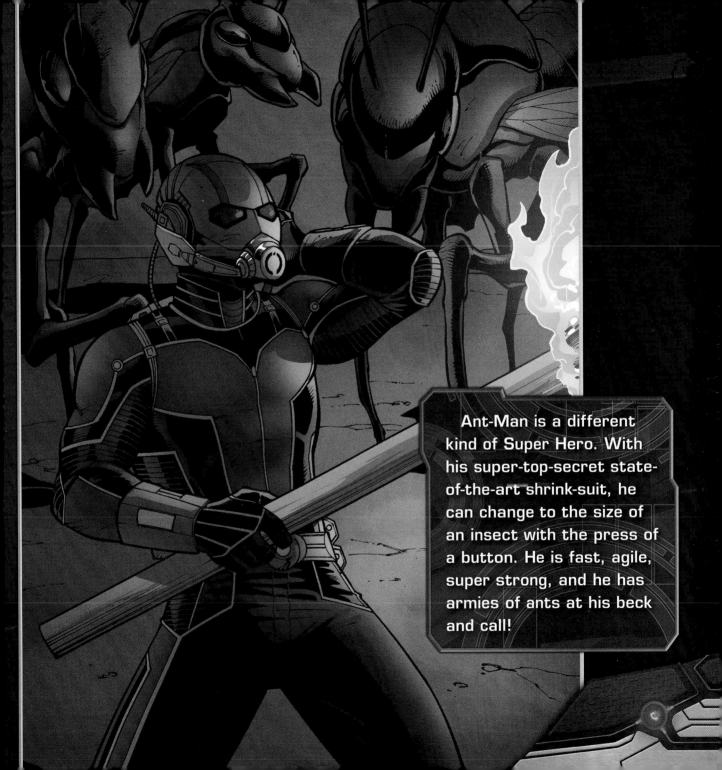

Ant-Man is a different kind of Super Hero. With his super-top-secret state-of-the-art shrink-suit, he can change to the size of an insect with the press of a button. He is fast, agile, super strong, and he has armies of ants at his beck and call!

It all started when Scott Lang found the suit. He was expecting to find money, so he was pretty disappointed to find some strange outfit. It looked like a cross between an old motorcycle jacket and a science experiment. It was just so...weird.

Scott had to try the suit on and see what it looked like. Besides, he knew his daughter, Cassie, would laugh when he told her about it. He and Cassie used to talk all the time about how cool it would be to be a Super Hero with a special costume, like Captain America or Iron Man. To Scott's surprise, the suit fit him perfectly!

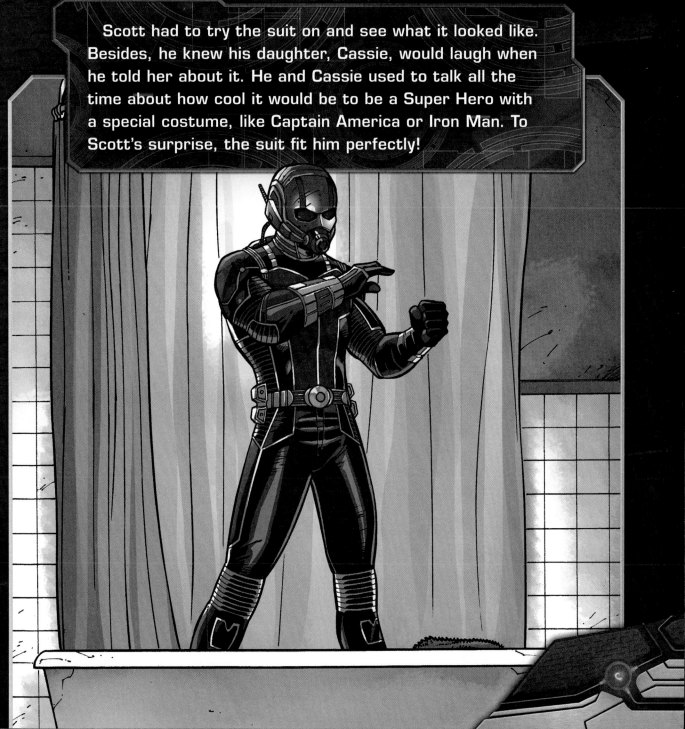

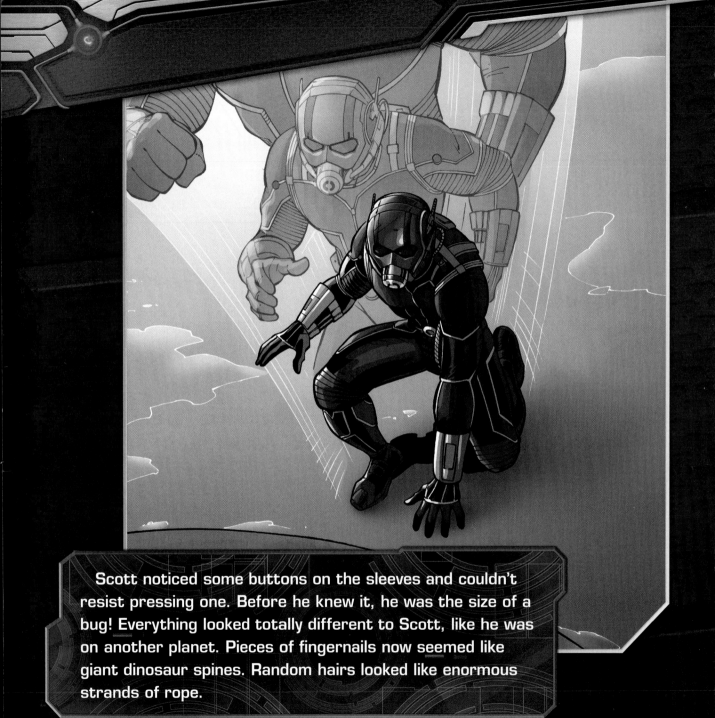

Scott noticed some buttons on the sleeves and couldn't resist pressing one. Before he knew it, he was the size of a bug! Everything looked totally different to Scott, like he was on another planet. Pieces of fingernails now seemed like giant dinosaur spines. Random hairs looked like enormous strands of rope.

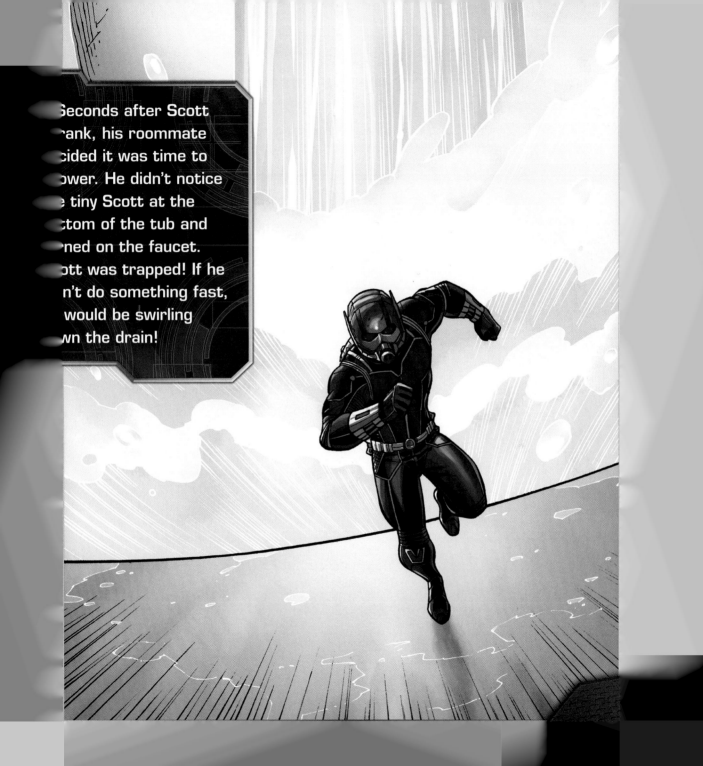

Seconds after Scott shrank, his roommate decided it was time to shower. He didn't notice the tiny Scott at the bottom of the tub and turned on the faucet. Scott was trapped! If he didn't do something fast, he would be swirling down the drain!

Luckily, with one small leap, Scott cleared the tidal wave of bathwater. He flew out of the tub and past his roommate!

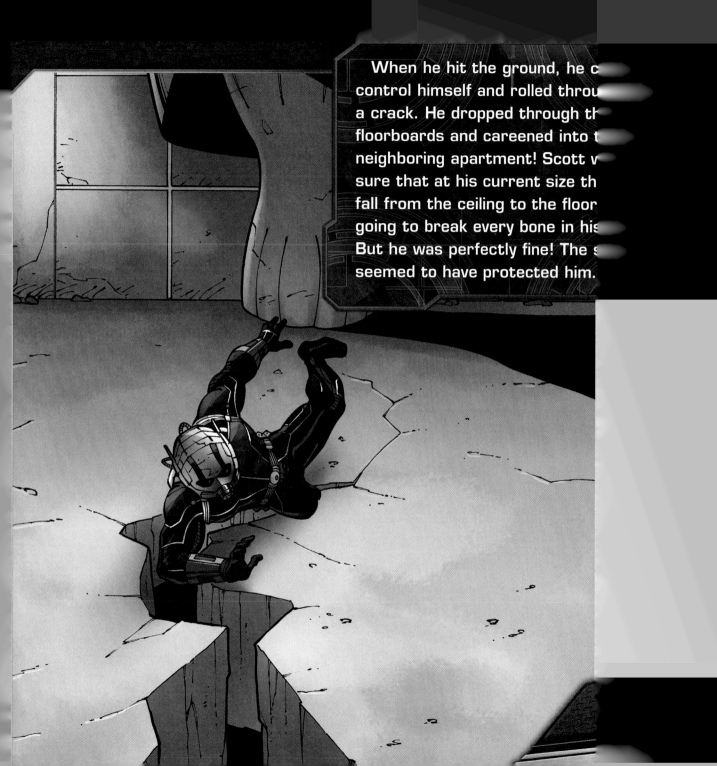

When he hit the ground, he c
control himself and rolled throu
a crack. He dropped through th
floorboards and careened into t
neighboring apartment! Scott v
sure that at his current size th
fall from the ceiling to the floor
going to break every bone in his
But he was perfectly fine! The s
seemed to have protected him.

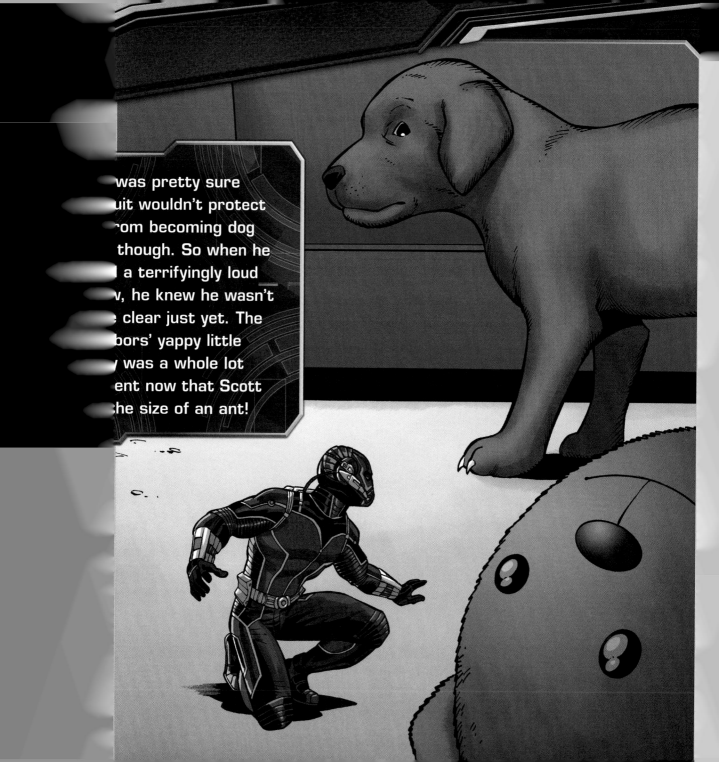

was pretty sure
uit wouldn't protect
om becoming dog
though. So when he
a terrifyingly loud
v, he knew he wasn't
e clear just yet. The
bors' yappy little
y was a whole lot
ent now that Scott
the size of an ant!

Scott jumped to and from pieces of furniture trying to shake the barking dog from his trail. Despite his best efforts, he couldn't lose him! He had to make a break for it.

ove toward
under the
ng to find
it he had no
. A woman
uming the
t where he
e tried to
e machine,
ew the odds
avor of him
a dust bunny.

Sure enough, the mechanical beast sucked him up and whipped him around with dirt and debris in what seemed like tornado-like winds. It was all a blur, but Scott got through A-OK! The helmet could sure take a beating! He thought he would be stuck in the vacuum forever but, luckily, the woman emptied the dust bag and Scott escaped.

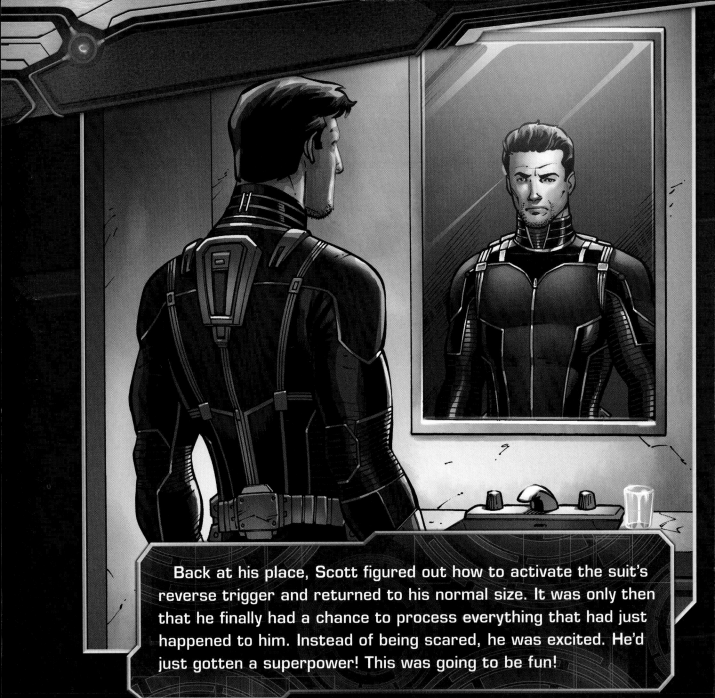

Back at his place, Scott figured out how to activate the suit's reverse trigger and returned to his normal size. It was only then that he finally had a chance to process everything that had just happened to him. Instead of being scared, he was excited. He'd just gotten a superpower! This was going to be fun!

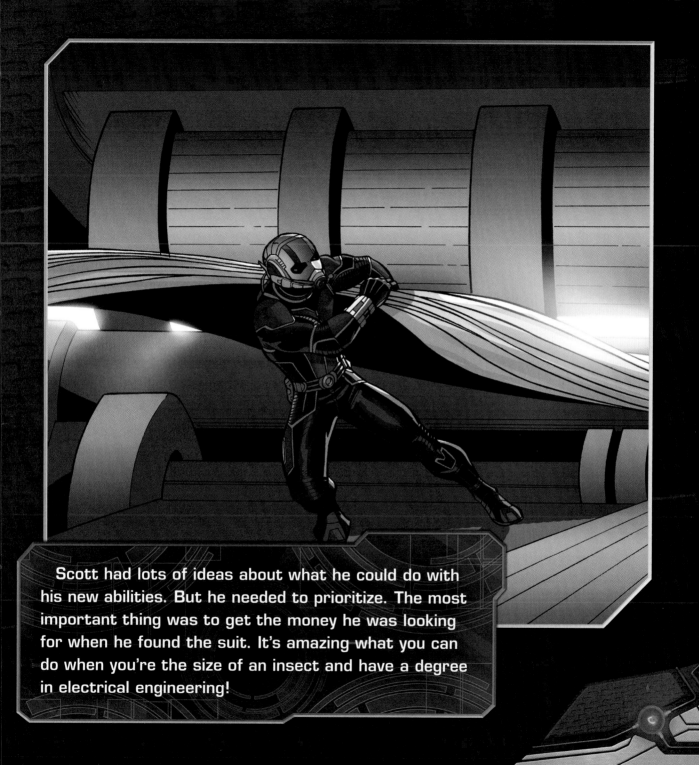

Scott had lots of ideas about what he could do with his new abilities. But he needed to prioritize. The most important thing was to get the money he was looking for when he found the suit. It's amazing what you can do when you're the size of an insect and have a degree in electrical engineering!

Scott had a lot of fun wearing the suit to help those in need, but when the novelty wore off, he realized how much he was missing Cassie. He still wasn't able to see his daughter as much as he wanted.

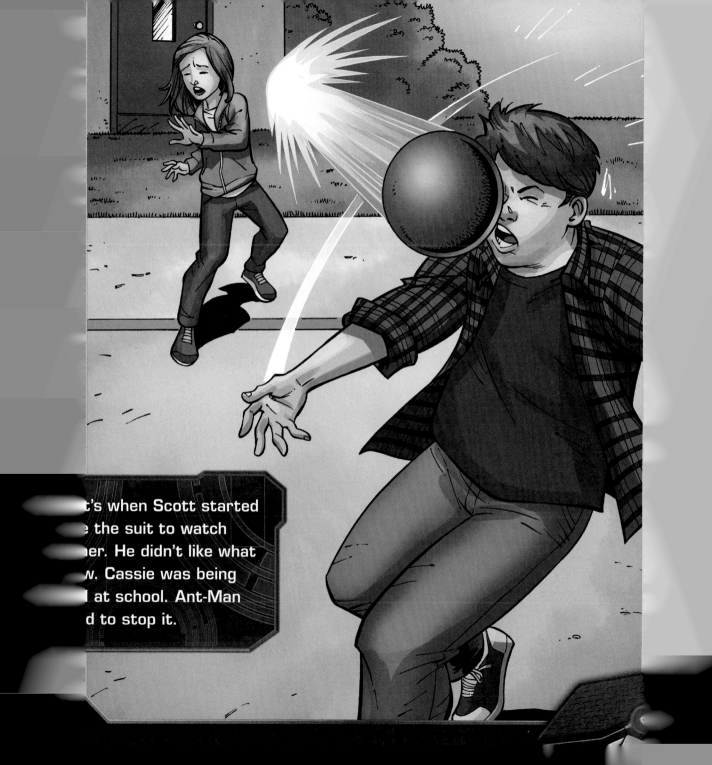

That's when Scott started to use the suit to watch over her. He didn't like what he saw. Cassie was being bullied at school. Ant-Man need to stop it.

Scott was so happy he could protect his little girl. He also felt pretty great standing up to the bully. Scott hoped the boy had learned his lesson.

Not long after, Scott was watching Cassie, when she said she'd heard some adults call her dad a bad man. Scott's heart dropped. He'd made some mistakes in the past but he'd changed. He wished Cassie could see the good he was doing. Then, from out of nowhere, Scott heard a voice as if it were in his own head:

"What do you think? Are you a bad man?"

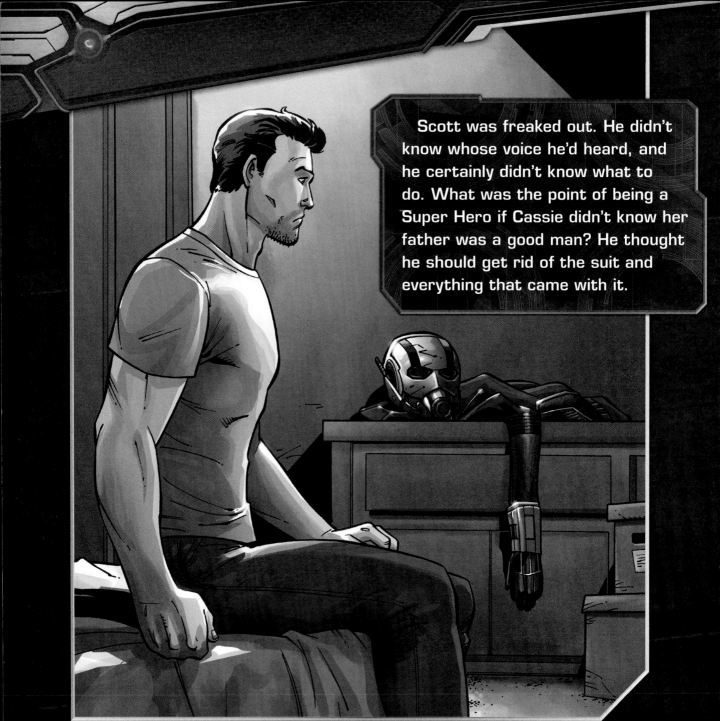

Scott was freaked out. He didn't know whose voice he'd heard, and he certainly didn't know what to do. What was the point of being a Super Hero if Cassie didn't know her father was a good man? He thought he should get rid of the suit and everything that came with it.

All he had to do was re[turn]
the suit to where he'd fo[und]
it, and after that, he cou[ld]
begin again. He needed t[o be]
a role model for Cassie.

The ants had other plans, though. Hours after Scott returned the suit, they brought it back to him. He was just sitting there, when all of a sudden, hundreds of ants, carrying the suit in its shrunken size, marched through a crack in the wall.

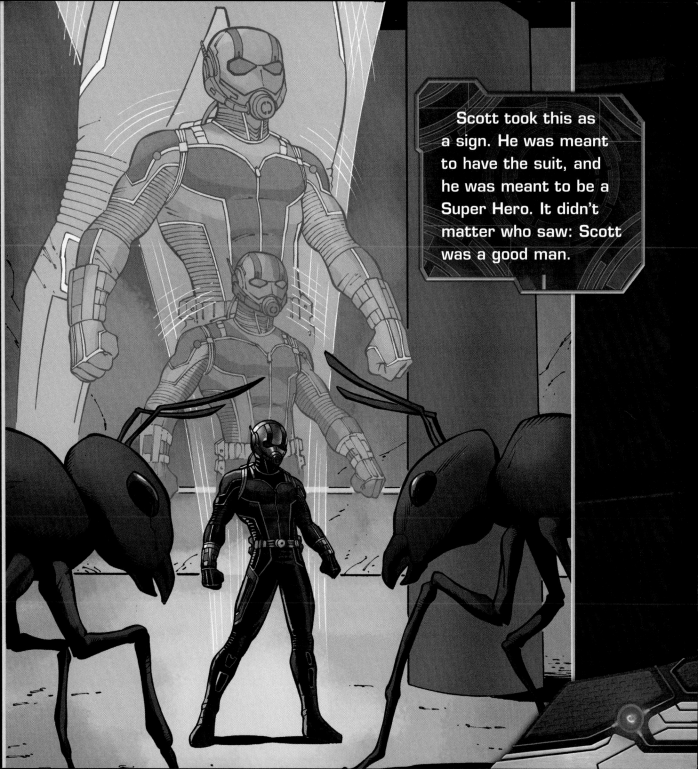

Scott took this as a sign. He was meant to have the suit, and he was meant to be a Super Hero. It didn't matter who saw: Scott was a good man.

Ant-Man not only protects Cassie, but the whole world. With Scott Lang's skills and the shrink-suit, nothing can stop him!

Directions: Punch out the mask, eyeholes, and string holes. Tie a string to each end of the mask. Tie the two strings together in the middle. Finally, place the mask on your face.

© 2015 MARVEL

MARVEL
ANT-MAN